Have No Fear, Chuckie's Here!

by Sarah Willson

illustrated by Robert Roper

Simon Spotlight/Nickelodeon

New York   London   Toronto   Sydney   Singapore

Based on the TV series *Rugrats*® created by Arlene Klasky, Gabor Csupo, and
Paul Germain as seen on Nickelodeon®

SIMON SPOTLIGHT
An imprint of Simon & Schuster Children's Publishing Division
1230 Avenue of the Americas
New York, New York 10020

Manufactured in the United States of America

First Edition

2 4 6 8 10 9 7 5 3 1

ISBN 0-689-84192-2

Hi. I'm Chuckie. Being an older brother comes with a lot of 'sponsibilities. Just the other day I saved my sister, Kimi, from being gobbled up by some froshus wild animals. I'll tell you all about it. If you feel scareded while I'm telling the story, just remember that it ends okay.

Me and my family were driving in the car. Suddenly the car stopped. We were in a big jungle. What are we doing *here?* I wondered. Maybe we'd runned outta gas. Then I heard my daddy say the wild beasties take kids for their dinner. My daddy is so brave, he didn't look scareded at all. I was glad he and my new mommy were there to protect me and Kimi.

But when I turned around, they were gone!
Me and Kimi were alone in the jungle.

"Kimi," I said. "We gots to get out of here and find Mommy and Daddy. The beasties will be here any minute." But did Kimi listen to me? A-course not.

The chickies were aborable all right. But where there are little chickies, there are big, hungry mommies and daddies. I had to save Kimi!

No sooner did I have her safe and sound than we were surrounded by big bunnies. They twitched their noses and hopped closer and closer. Maybe they thought my hair was made of carrots. I didn't want to be no bunny's dinner.

The next thing we saw were some duckies. Kimi thought they were cruddly. But I've been around the blocks a few times. I know what other things can be swimmin' in those duckie ponds—slimy sea creeptures, for egg-sample.

We rolled away just in time. I was starting to think we would never see our mommy and daddy again, when suddenly I spotted them! But standing right in front of us were some giant sheeps. If you had seen the way they were staring at us, chewing with their mouthses, like they were thinking about how yummy we looked, you'd have prob'ly done the same thing I did.

"Run, Kimi!" I yelled. "This way!"

We almost got to our mommy and daddy. But then I saw the most horriblest creeptures of all. They had Kimi surrounded. I hid my eyes. I couldn't look.

And it was then I gots ta thinkin'. There comes a time in a baby's life when he realizes he can't hide every time he feels like it. I knew I had to stand up to those beasties if it was the lastest thing I done—and it prob'ly *was* going to be the lastest thing I done.

I stooped down and grabbed up the first thing I saw. "Save yourself, Kimi!" I yelled to my sister. "Run for it!"

As she ran for cover, I turned toward the creeptures.

"Take that, you big beasties!" I yelled.

I closed my eyes, waiting for the worst. Then I felt something tugging at my hand. Those big animals were nibblin' on something. Was it me? I opened my eyes. No! They were eating the grass and flowers I was holding! I was screaded, but I fed those big creeptures till they were full.

When I thought the toast was clear, I ran for it. "I'll be okay. I'll be okay. I'll be okay," I said to myself. I ran into my daddy's arms. I was okay. And so was Kimi, thanks to me.

So that's the story of how I saved my sister, Kimi. She doesn't know how dangered she was, and I don't think I'll ever tell her. I wouldn't want her to be scareded.